G000253532

SAFARI

Safari

OWEN SHEERS

HAY FESTIVAL PRESS

2007

Published by
Hay Festival Press
The Drill Hall, 25 Lion Street
Hay HR3 5AD, United Kingdom

www.hayfestival.com

ISBN-10 0 9547168 7 6
ISBN-13 978 0 9547168 7 5

1,100 copies (of which 100 have been
numbered and signed by the author)
have been printed on Simili Japon paper
and casebound by Cambridge University Press

Designed and typeset in Ehrhardt
by Five Seasons Press, Hereford

*Profits from the Hay Festival Press fund the educational
programmes of the Festivals of Literature Charitable Trust*

TWO STORIES

OF THE FOUR BROTHELS they visited that morning, Little Rose's Place was clearly the most organized. A metallic blue pick-up was parked at the foot of the stone steps leading up to the entrance. The truck had been pimped; black windows, thick tyres, chrome bumpers and an orange logo running the length of each side: *Bad Boyz Security*. Two men slouched in the cab. Another four sat in the open back. All of them wore sunglasses, thin vests, jeans and flip-flops. When Peter and Tiisetso got out of their own car and walked past the truck six pairs of eyes followed them up the steps and into the lobby. Peter saw the barrel of a shotgun resting between the legs of the driver like the nose of a loyal dog dozing in the footwell.

They'd found the lobby itself empty other than for a woman standing in a barred-off kiosk against the far wall. A plastic sign tied to the bars told them to *Please leave bags and guns here.* Opposite the kiosk a pair of soundproofed double doors muffled a distant bass beat. Above these doors Peter could make out another sign in faded ochre paint, parts of its letters chipped away by peeling plaster: *Dress Code for all Customers is Smart Casual.* Directly facing them was a corkboard on which he noticed a printed sheet of paper pinned in the left hand corner: *Calling all Little Rose ladies—Meeting tonight with management. Agenda @ meeting.* Yes, Little Rose, whoever she was, obviously ran a very different place to the others they'd seen that morning.

It wasn't just these signs that eased the fear that had curdled within Peter for most of the morning. It was also the light; a flat white fluorescence from two humming strips on the ceiling reflected off the white linoleum tiles of the floor. There had been no signs in those other places. And there had been no light either, other than what scraps of sunlight made it through the few wire-laced, shit-smeared windows. Stepping in to each of those places off the bright Johannesburg streets, Peter had stepped into night. A night of shadows on shadows, flies tapping and buzzing at ankle level, and all of it wrapped in the heavy scents of piss and marijuana.

'I wouldn't call them brothels, as such,' Tiisetso had said as they'd driven towards the first of these places. 'Squats. That's all they are. Squats where the girls rent a room for a few weeks before moving on. New is good, so they always move on.'

'Who from?' he'd asked her. 'If it's a squat, who do they rent from?'

'Whoever owns them at the time. Someone always does. There's always a man taking the money. It changes.'

Yes, Peter had thought, looking out at the passing streets of Hillsborough, it does. When had he first seen this part of town? Fifteen years ago? He'd come to a party soon after he'd arrived in the country. His first time in Africa. Twenty-five years old, smooth-faced and charged with an angry energy. Back then, standing in that lushly-furnished room, a glass of champagne in his hand, the party had felt like his first mission; infiltrating the enemy's headquarters, subversion from within. These elegant cliffs of houses they were passing now had then been home to the people he'd hated. Rich white South Africans, indulgent and arrogant in their mansion blocks on the hill. Living above it all. But he'd shaken them up, hadn't he? Both that night and with the pieces he'd written in the months afterwards, until the authorities caught up with him and sent him packing.

Tiisetso stopped at a set of lights. Two young men were washing a police car pulled up at the kerb. A blocky 1980s beat box on the pavement accompanied their wiping and brushing with a steady drum 'n' bass percussion. Peter watched them, the energy with which they splashed the windscreen with a bucket of water before swiping it off again with their sponges in straight-arm arcs.

'They only come here to have their vehicles washed,' Tiisetso said, tutting through her teeth and flicking her chin in the direction of the boys working over the patrol car's bonnet. 'You won't see them here otherwise.'

The lights changed and Tiisetso drove on, deeper into this place where, fifteen years ago, the chief of police's daughter had once lived, and where now the police wouldn't even show their faces after dark. Peter carried on looking out the window. They had all day. He didn't want to ask too many questions yet. So he just watched as they drove past the pavements, the cut-price shops, the street-sellers. Everyone they passed was a man. Tiisetso, driving beside him, had been the only woman he'd seen.

For a few moments they just stood in the lobby of Little Rose's Place doing nothing.

Perhaps she's as relieved as me, Peter had thought. Relieved to have come across a bit of order after seeing so much chaos. He was breathing through his mouth to avoid scenting the air. The smell of that first place had made him gag. He'd felt the acid taste of vomit rise in his throat and he hadn't wanted to risk it again. Now, though, encouraged by the signs, the linoleum, even the pimped security truck outside, he took a breath through his nose. The smell was of pine-scented floor cleaner with a faint hint of spilt beer lurking beneath. He turned to Tiisetso.

'So, what's the plan?'

'The manager should be here to see us. He's been working with the centre. He even sponsored one girl. At the beginning. When we started.'

She looked at her watch, walked over to

the woman in the kiosk and spoke to her in Xhosa. She turned back to Peter.

'Stay here for a moment. I won't be long.'

As she pushed through the double doors a brief wash of the music beyond flooded the lobby, diminishing again as the doors swung, first past each other and then closed.

⁂

It was the first time she'd left him all day. Obviously he'd been right to feel safer here. She was an impressive woman, this Tiisetso. The PR girl for the British NGO funding her project had said as much. Been one of these girls herself apparently; got caught up in it straight off the train, like so many of them. The tracks fed into the city from all over the country, bringing in a daily supply of new rural girls looking to make some money. Not that they'd had this in mind. Peter thought again of the rooms Tiisetso had shown him. How small they were. Small, dark and bare. A chequered mattress, maybe a bed. A single crucifix on an otherwise naked wall. Then he thought of the spaces from which so many of them would have come. The wide velds, the long plains, the broad hills. The comparison, the idea of this exchange of light for dark, rural for city, space for enclosure made him feel better about the piece he'd write on this. Not just because he was starting to see a shape to it, how it might work, but also because it reminded him he really cared about what was happening here. So he'd make sure it was a good one, a bloody good piece to shake them up, just as the ones he'd written fifteen years ago had. If he could find someone to take it. The usual editors he'd worked with in the past hadn't sounded too keen.

'AIDS in South Africa. Christ, Peter, where's the story? Hardly new, is it? What's the angle? Is there a date to hook it on?'

That's when he'd called the PR girl again and she'd told him about Tiisetso's own past. That had helped. The neatness of it. Reformed prostitute caring for the girls no one else will. And the fact it was working. Five thousand girls helped by the outreach programme. Seventy put through school last year. Working despite unhelpful statements from government ministers about beetroot and showers either curing or preventing HIV. It hadn't been enough to secure a commission but it was enough to muster sufficient interest for the NGO to risk flying him out. And God it had felt good to be back. It had been too long, that's what he'd told himself when he stepped off the plane and felt Africa again: felt her smack him in the face with her heat, felt her ease him down and rev him up, at one and the same time. When he'd taken a walk through the city at night and felt, once again, the purity of her rawness.

But then this morning, as Tiisetso had driven them to the first place, his spirit for it all had flagged again. He suspected he knew why, although he didn't like to admit it.

'Matt Damon, Madonna, I've shown them all around the project. Clinton's people have come to have a look too.'

He'd nodded, raised his eyebrows to convey a suitable level of impression. Then asked the most aggressive question he could think of.

'But the infection rates are only dropping because so many are dying, isn't that right?

And although the punters use condoms now, the girls' boyfriends won't. It's a bit of a losing battle isn't it?'

Tiisetso had flicked her eyes at the rear view mirror, indicated and taken a left turn. He thought she wasn't going to answer him, but half-way up the next street she'd simply said, 'Don't worry, I'll show you something different. There were places I couldn't take them. There are just two of us.'

They'd driven on to the first place in silence. He'd been angry at her for suggesting he was only interested in his story. That simply wasn't true. He badly wanted to write about what she was doing here, what she'd achieved. But not, he admitted to himself now, standing in the lobby of Little Rose's Place, as much as he wanted to be her, to have her impact, her access.

He wandered over to the notice board. There was little else on it other than the meeting flyer. A card for *Bad Boyz Security*, a missing persons poster and another printed sheet giving details of Tiisetso's project. He looked into the barred kiosk but the woman had gone. He was entirely on his own. It was what he'd wanted all day, after the sheer terror of those other places, the menace of the streets and the cloying heat and sweat smell of other people. But now it was the last thing he wanted, so, giving one of the soundproof doors a hefty shove, he stepped into the room beyond.

Once again he had stepped into night. It took a moment for his eyes to adjust but when they did all he could see was the curved edge of a bar and a group of male heads silhouetted against the pink and blue sweeping lights of a disco. The music was louder than he'd expected, and not what he'd expected. *Time after Time* by Cyndi Lauper was stretching the speakers to their full capacity. He hadn't moved far from the door and, now he was inside, he didn't want to.

He must have felt her watching him, that's what he told himself afterwards. Why else would he have turned to look into that part of the room? It was unlit, a corner, nothing could have been there. Except of course, there had been. Her, leaning against the end of the bar's curve, arms folded, watching him. He took a step towards her and leaned in.

'Hello.'

Maybe she hadn't heard him. The music

was so loud and the expression of her face hadn't changed. He leant in again, feeling a little ridiculous.

'My name's Peter.'

'Hello Peter.'

Her voice didn't suit her body. She was fat. There was no other way of describing her. Her arms were fat, her neck was fat, and her jeans stretched over her stomach as taut as a sail in a full wind. But her voice was thin. Thin and quiet. And yet, unlike Peter, she didn't seem to have to shout for him to be able to hear her.

'And yours?' he asked.

'Rosebud.'

He nodded, smiling.

'And what do you do here, Rosebud?'

For the first time her face conveyed a connection. Raising both her eyebrows and her chin slightly, she cocked her head to one side. Peter thought he saw the ghost of a smile.

'I have sex with men for money. What are you doing here?'

Of course she does, Peter thought, it's a bloody brothel you idiot. Why had he thought she wouldn't? Was it her size? All the girls he'd seen today had been small, almost childlike. He smiled again, a tighter, close-lipped smile, and kept nodding.

'I'm a journalist. Do you know Tiisetso?'

She raised her eyebrows again, higher this time, to indicate she did.

'Well, I'm writing about her and her project.'

Her eyes were looking straight into his but she was giving nothing else away.

'About the work she does.'

The rest of the bar seemed to have melted

into the lights and music. He glanced around and could just see smoke curling through the disco beams, vague shapes, but no other people. Turning back to Rosebud he tried again.

‘Where are you from, Rosebud?’

For the first time she looked away from him. He felt as if she’d been judging him all this time and somehow he’d just failed. She didn’t bother looking back when she answered.

‘Botswana. I’m from Botswana.’

‘Ah, I know Botswana,’ he said, trying to pare the eagerness to please out of his voice. ‘I wrote a piece about the San, the Bushmen, a few years back.’

Very slowly, she turned her head to look at him again.

‘And what did you have to say about the San, Peter?’ She said his name like it was a needle with which she was about to pierce him.

'Well, it was about how they were being treated, I suppose. About that fence that went up across their hunting grounds. The one all the migrating animals died against.'

She was still looking at him. He waited, but again there was no response.

'The Botswanan government weren't too happy about it. They banned me.'

He paused again. She blinked and sighed, her chest held within her folded arms expanding and falling like a single wave long-grown over miles of ocean.

'Put my name on a list in an internal newsletter. Told me I wasn't welcome there again. Never been back since.'

'Why are you here?'

After waiting for a response for so long, her question took him by surprise. She asked it as if he hadn't just been speaking to her at all.

'I told you, I'm a journalist, I'm writing—'

'Yes, I know. About Tiisetso. But why, Peter? Why have you come here to write about Tiisetso? To write about us?'

'It's important. An important story. She's doing important work.' He heard himself and couldn't quite believe this was the answer he was giving, but it was true. That was why he was there. 'People have got tired of AIDS stories, so any new ones are, well, important.'

She smiled again, this time with a shake of the head.

'This is not a new story, Peter. It is the oldest story there is.'

He didn't answer, just looked back at her, frowning.

'Where you are from, Peter, you have a house?'

'Yes, yes I do.'

'And a wife?'

'No, I'm not married. I have a girl-friend.'

'And she lives with you?'

'No, she has her own place.'

'So you just see her when you want sex?'

'No! Christ, no. No. We see each other all the time.'

She looked away again, into the lights and the smoke. Peter looked away as well. Where the hell was Tiisetso? She said she'd only be gone for a minute.

'So what do you think your writing will do?'

He turned back to look at her. The music was giving him a headache and he wished he'd stayed in the lobby.

'Do? Well, I hope it'll help, I suppose. In some way. Raise awareness.'

'And will that make something happen, Peter? Will that make things better here?'

'Christ,' he swept a hand over his face and through his hair. 'I don't know. I hope so.' He paused, then began nodding, slowly at first then more energetically, more to himself than to her. 'Actually, yes, it will. I think if enough pieces are written, if enough attention is paid, something will happen. Yes.'

She was still looking away, but now she turned back to him once more.

'Why don't you take me home with you?'

'Pardon?'

'If you want to make a difference. Take me to your country. Marry me. That will help.'

He laughed. 'Yes, I suppose it might. But only you.'

'Isn't that something? Better than just maybe helping many?'

He looked into her face and realised she was serious. About something, if not about her proposal of marriage.

'Look,' he said, glancing over his shoulder for Tiisetso again. 'I should get going. I'm meant to be meeting the manager.'

Now it was her turn to laugh. A short, breathy hiccup, but a laugh nonetheless. She looked away again, scanning her eyes over the room before bringing them back to rest on his.

'I think you are a good man, Peter. But I do not think you should be here. I do not think you understand.'

She held his eye as she said this, and held it still in the music and smoke-filled silence between them afterwards.

What the hell did she mean? Don't

understand? Peter felt an old anger rise in his chest the way the acid and bile had risen in his throat earlier. He'd seen those places this morning. He'd seen this whole area fifteen years ago. Christ, he'd been here during apartheid and then come back to cover its end. His writing had played a part then, hadn't it? Of course he bloody understood. More so than she did. He wasn't the one selling his body in a shithole like this. A shithole in a once beautiful area where they now celebrate New Year by throwing fridges out of the windows. Where the streets are empty of women and full of men on the prowl, the make, or both. A shithole like this full of girls with HIV who won't take their drugs because their ministers say all they need is a good meal or, even better, a quick shower after sex to stop them getting it in the first place. So yes, actually, he does understand. He does fucking understand. He understands that he was bloody delighted when apartheid died, but that something's gone wrong since. Something has gone very, very fucking wrong.

⁂

The butt of the shotgun hit him in his kidneys. He went down before he even realised he'd been hit, before he realised he'd been shouting at the top of his voice. Two pairs of large hands dragged him to his feet. He felt he was going to be sick. A man's face wearing sunglasses swam into view. And then she was there. Rosebud, prising the hands off him. Pushing him, no, leaning him against the bar. Her passive face suddenly animated with Xhosa. The hands went away. The sunglasses went away.

The double doors opened and swung shut behind him, feeding thinner and thinner pages of light into the room. And then, from somewhere, there was Tiisetso.

'Oh, Peter. I'm sorry. I didn't know where you'd got to. Let's get you back to the hotel.'

Now it was her hands, smaller, lighter, on his arm, leading him towards the double doors. He turned to look for Rosebud. He couldn't see her and yet, as they moved away from the dark corner, he heard her.

'Go home, Peter. Go home. And don't worry, I will stay here. Waiting for something to happen.'

A Bird in the Hand

A LATE ARRIVAL in a new country. It was a pleasure he'd learnt as a child. Heavy with sleep in the back seat of his parents' car, or slumped in a coach, his forehead resting against the thrumming window. And then, as the suitcases were unloaded, dark cubist sculptures assembled on the cooling tarmac, he'd step out and look at their destination, unknown under night. In the distance, the pale promise of a beach. Nearer, a lighter patch of dark that may be a pool or perhaps a sandpit. The inky blocks of the buildings against a blue-black sky. Somewhere, the sound of the sea. It was these half-arrivals he'd enjoyed, incomplete until the morning when the landscape of his holiday would be revealed in all its honesty under a brilliant Mediterranean sun.

It's traces of this childhood sensation he feels again now as he bunches the curtain pleats in his hand and looks out of the hotel's French windows, through the white balcony and into the square below. Early coffee drinkers sit under the plane trees, the gravel around them dappled by the sun through their leaves. Looking above these trees he can see a white clock tower against a blue sky and beyond that magnolia stucco houses piling over each other up the hill. Without looking back down into the square, at the men's jumpers, the women's scarves, he knows the blue sky is cold. An autumn morning, not a summer one.

Still holding the curtain open with one hand he reaches for the handle with his other. The mechanism gives with a thick clunk.

He pushes the door open, just enough to let a blade of air into the room and to allow the sound of the pigeons cooing and bubbling in the eaves above to filter down to him.

He turns to look at her. A shaft of sunlight is cutting across her back, over the puckered sheets, but her head is left in the dusk of the room and she is still asleep. He hadn't seen her for a week when they'd met last night. He'd been away on business and she'd been working in London. They'd both been busy and over the seven days apart the phone calls had grown tauter down the line. So perhaps it was no surprise he'd been disappointed. Not to look at her, he was never disappointed in that way, and as usual, he'd admired her as she walked through the airport bustle, her dark hair tied back from her face, the way he liked it, allowing her tendon-carved neck room to breathe.

He'd watched her make her way towards him, looking for him, and he'd seen again how other men's eyes caught on her. But then she had seen him, and he had known, right away, he was going to be disappointed. And already he was steeling himself, hoping her first words would be kind, that she would offer him her lips. But they were not and she had not, and like a glass palace erected on weak foundations he'd felt the weekend fissure on this fragile beginning. It was a fault of his, he knew that now, but he couldn't help it. Beginnings were important to him. First words, opening sentences. The potential they held.

He's looking at her. She can tell he is, something in the fabric of his sounds. The pause in movement. A streak of sunlight is falling across her back but its band of warmth feels like his eyes, looking at her. She knows what he'll be thinking too. Last night. She was tired, had to cut her last meeting short. The tube and train were packed, a press of flesh and the smell of offices. He'd forgotten to tell her the flight number. She couldn't find the right desk. She didn't trust him.

Then there'd been the flight. No seat allocation and a repainted plane that was obviously too old, flip-up ashtrays in the arms of the seats. The turbulence unnerved her, as he knew it always did, but still, she knows he won't be thinking about any of that.

She stirs, partly to disrupt this chain of thought and partly to show him she's awake. She feels his weight on the edge of the bed, his hand, still cold from the window, on her shoulder.

'What time is it?' She speaks into the pillow, quietly, eyes closed.

'Just past eight.'

'You're up early.'

'I thought I'd take a walk, find a paper.'

'Mmm, that'd be nice. What's it like out?'

'Nice. Cold I think. I won't be long.'

'OK.'

His fingers slide away. 'Love you.'

'Mmm, you too.'

She listens to his steps over the carpet, the rustle of his coat off the back of the chair and the click, sweep, click of the door, opening and closing. The sound of him fades down the stairway, and she turns over, sighing, shifting her head down the pillow until the sunbeam catches her face and she feels its heat, sudden and sparkling under her closed eyes.

They see the bird as they are leaving the hotel. The day that had begun so coolly has found a ripe September warmth and the drinkers in the square at the front are in T-shirts and dresses now. But they are leaving by the rear entrance, through a pale walled courtyard and into a quiet narrow back street, bleached bright in the sun. Which is where they see the pigeon.

'Is it dead?'

As if it can hear her the bird lifts a wing from its side and makes a pathetic shuffle in the pale dust.

'It must have been hit by a car,' he says, looking behind him, up the narrow slope between the whitewashed houses. Further down, by the river, he can hear cars, can imagine their hot, sticky seats, their thick gasoline haze in this heat, but here, there are no cars.

She removes her sunglasses and goes towards the bird.

'I think its wing is broken.'

'And its leg, by the look of it.'

The pigeon lies on its side, motionless in the dust but for the twitching of its grey wrinkled eyelids.

She looks at him.

'We should do something.'

He looks down at the bird. The feathers round its neck are purple and blue, as if they've been glazed in a kiln.

'I don't know. I think it's pretty much dead.'

But still he bends and picks it up, surprised by how light it feels. The bird does nothing and is limp in his hands as he carries it to the side of the road where rain from the night before has puddled in a shallow gutter.

'Maybe it just needs some water.'

He lays it within reach of the old rain, then stands. They both look at it for a moment. He notices the thinness of its red legs, she the way its feathers overlap, a fan of greys and whites, the colours of a winter sea. He touches the small of her back.

'I think the shops might shut early on a Saturday here.'

They turn away from the bird and walk up the slope that will take them, via the back streets, into the centre of the small town. The sun is hot on the backs of their necks, and he squints in its glare while she settles her sunglasses back on the bridge of her nose.

He wants to have a picnic before the wedding. On his walk earlier he saw a spot on the far bank of the river that looked perfect. Shaded, soft grass, unbleached by the long summer's heat. 'It's a perfect spot,' he'd told her, 'perfect.'

When they return they are carrying plastic bags of shopping: cheese, sliced ham, fruit, a bottle of wine and two flaking baguettes. All the way down the slope towards the hotel he watches the motionless body of the pigeon.

'It's dead,' he says, pushing open the gate into the courtyard.

'Yes,' she replies, a trace of relief in her voice, 'yes, it is.'

The grass by the river is not as soft as it had looked from the other bank, but patchy and surprisingly sharp and rigid. It sticks into their skin through his cotton trousers and her summer skirt. The sun has risen higher since he saw the place earlier, and the generous blanket of shade has been reduced to dark scraps over the scuffed ground. The cork crumbles in the bottle and flies, drawn to the water, light again and again on their faces and necks. The air tastes of traffic.

He does not know it, but it's this grass that makes him doubt their love. It has unsettled his projection of what his life should be like. But instead of blaming the grass, or himself, he blames her. So, as they sit there in the still mid-afternoon heat, he finds himself imagining again a parallel life, in which he is sitting here with another woman with whom the sharpness of the grass, the flies, the uncomfortable heat, the crumbled cork, would not matter. And as she lies back against him and he strokes the pale skin on the underside of her wrist, he decides, as he has done a hundred times before, that he will leave her, knowing, in the same seam of thought, that he will never have the courage to do so.

Lying there with her eyes closed, feeling the nail of his finger drag up and down her arm, she knows, once more, what he is thinking. She has come to recognise the patterns, the ebb and flow of his affection and over the years she has been able to chart these tides, cross-referencing them against events. In this way she has become a cartographer of his emotions, but now the effort of navigating them, of knowing the waters, is draining her. The give and the take. The becalmed threat of his love. Recently, it has made her think of an interview she once saw on television. A freed hostage on a breakfast-show sofa, an inset photograph of him dishevelled and bearded above his now clean-shaven face. She'd sat on the edge of her bed, one leg of her tights pulled up to her thigh, the other rolled over her hand like a glove, as he'd described to the host how his guards took him out each morning, to execute him. It was the same pattern every day—blindfolded, hands tied, kneeling in the dusty courtyard, the metallic click and slide of the guns cocking behind his head. And then nothing, just the hum and scramble of distant downtown traffic. Everything building to an end that never came. Eventually, he explained, his desire swung on the fulcrum of that repeated moment, on those kinetic seconds, from life to death. And all he wanted after that was the end, no longer the potential of reprieve, just the end that never came.

It is as she's brushing sparks of grass from his back by the courtyard gate that they see the dead bird move. At first he thinks it's the wind, catching against the grain of its feathers. But then its wing twitches again, and when he goes over to it the wrinkled grey eyelids part across a tiny black pearl.

He bends to the bird, feeling the dampness of the sweat behind his knees.

'I should kill it,' he says, not looking at her.

He listens to her steps through the courtyard, the opening and closing of the hotel's door. And then it is quiet. It is the afternoon, the cars are parked beside the river and most of the town is asleep. The passageway where he crouches seems impossibly bright, the flat glare of the sun reflecting off the whitewashed walls. He picks the pigeon up with his hands about its wings and carries it to the other side of the street where the wall is in shade and a creeping plant hangs down from a window-box of geraniums above.

He knows what to do. His grandfather showed him how to break chickens' necks when he was a boy, but still he looks at the bird for a long time, weighing its life in his mind. Eventually he goes to pick it up, but he is slow to close his hands around its wings and the pigeon, that had been so limp before, flaps and struggles against him, sensing his intention. Surprised by its sudden energy he drops it to the floor where it tries to shuffle away from him, collapsing repeatedly on its broken leg and wing.

He reaches for it again, holding it with more resolve this time, so although he can feel its delicate muscles straining under his fingers, it is still, its head hanging limp over his knuckles. He places the forefinger of his right hand at its throat and the pad of his thumb against the back of its neck, his fingers sinking through the feathers until they are almost touching either side of the thin vertebrae. A tremor of breath runs under the finger at its throat as he places his other hand over its head, smothering its beak and eyes in a loose fist. Pressing down with his thumb, as if breaking a twig, he tightens his hand over the bird's head and pulls and twists. Its neck doesn't break and the bird struggles, opening its beak inside his palm with a thin gasp. One panicked wing breaks free and as he gathers it back under his fingers he catches a glimpse of its wide-open eyes. Closing his own, he tries again, pulling violently as he wrings the bird like a dishcloth. When he opens them again he doesn't understand why his hands are so far apart until he looks down at the headless body and sees the thin gulping stream of blood spurting against the white paint of the wall.

He jerks back, opening his hands and dropping the decapitated pigeon. Its body flaps and convulses for several seconds, the tips of its wings writing in the dust. The head, lying in its own dark puddle, blinks twice, then opens its beak and lets out a long hiss, its thin pink and grey tongue appearing for a moment, then falling away again as the eyelids close and flatten.

Standing, he nudges the body, then the head, up against the wall with his shoe. He looks up the empty street then turns and walks into the courtyard, holding his lightly spattered hands before him, like a man who has dipped his arms in acid and is afraid of burning himself with his own touch.

That evening they watch their friends marry at a small rural chateau. The bride wears a red silk dress she has made herself and every time he looks at her he sees the splash of blood against the white wall. They sit together through the ceremony, holding hands, and with the priest's sermon as her backdrop, she decides to bring about the end herself. She is tired of waiting and although she says nothing to him, he already knows. Just as the bird sensed the difference between his killing and carrying hands, so he senses the change in her brief embrace. After dinner in the chateau's open courtyard he sits at a deserted table, stunned in its resonance, while she dances in the opposite room. Waiters move about him, lighting candles, and the sun dips perfectly through the entrance archway, firing up the stained-glass windows of the chapel. As he watches her spin and dance, appearing and disappearing between the windows and columns around the courtyard, the pigeons call to each other in the eaves and fly in scatterings across the square of darkening sky above him. He watches and he marvels as he never has done before at what miracles they are. At the elegance of their swooping movements, and at the fragility of their common lives, held so precariously within those thin bone cages that break so easily.

Other titles in the
Hay Festival Press uniform series

available from www.hayfestival.com

BOTTLE
Margaret Atwood
2004

A NIGHT OFF FOR PRUDENTE DE MORAES
Louis de Bernières
2004

MEETING CÉZANNE
Michael Morpurgo
2005

TWO STORIES
Jeanette Winterson
2005

LONG AGO YESTERDAY
Hanif Kureishi
2006

TANGLED WEB
Doris Lessing
2007

THE HAPPINESS OF BLOND PEOPLE
Elif Shafak
2007